Copyright © 1994 by Christopher Denise

Published by Philomel Books, a division of The Putnam &

Grosset Group, 200 Madison Avenue, New York, NY 10016.

All rights reserved. This book, or parts thereof,

may not be reproduced in any form without permission

in writing from the publisher.

Philomel Books, Reg. U.S. Pat. & Tm. Off.

Published simultaneously in Canada.

Printed in Hong Kong by South China Printing Co. (1988) Ltd.

Lettering by David Gatti

The text is set in Caslon No. 3.

The artist used acrylic on gessoed watercolor paper

to create the illustrations for this book.

Library of Congress Cataloging-in-Publication Data

Denise, Christopher.   The fool of the world and the flying ship /

illustrated by Christopher Denise.   p.   cm.

Summary: When the Tsar proclaims that he will marry his

daughter to the one who brings him a flying ship,

the Fool of the World sets out to try his luck.

[1. Folklore—Russia.] I. Title.

PZ8.1.D454Fo   1994   398.21'0947—dc20

92-2656 CIP AC

1 3 5 7 9 10 8 6 4 2

First Impression

THE FOOL OF THE WORLD and THE FLYING SHIP

A RUSSIAN FOLKTALE FROM

THE SKAZKI OF POLEVOI

ILLUSTRATED BY

CHRISTOPHER DENISE

PHILOMEL BOOKS • NEW YORK

For Lynn

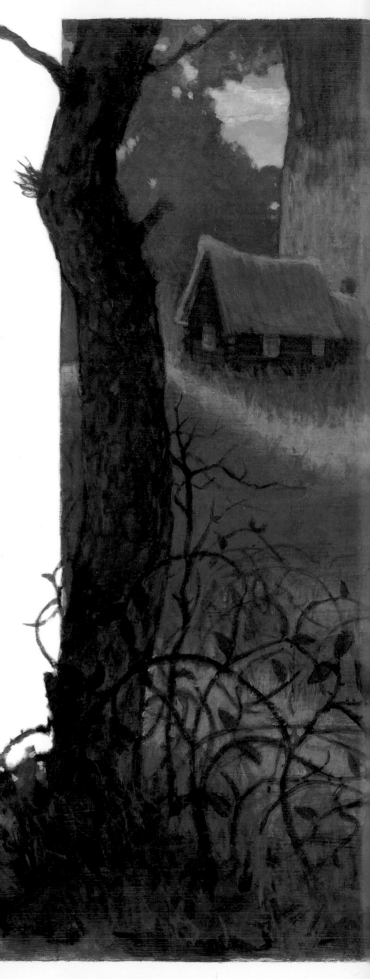

There was once upon a time an old peasant and his old wife, and they had three sons. Two were clever, but the third was a fool. The old woman loved the first two and quite spoiled them, but the latter was always harshly treated.

One day all three heard that a proclamation had come from the Tsar that said:

Whoever builds a ship that can fly,
to him I will give my daughter,
the Tsarevna, as wife.

The elder brothers resolved to go and seek their fortunes, and they begged a blessing from their parents. The mother made ready their things, and gave them something to eat and a flask of wine for the journey. And the Fool began to beg and beg them to send him off too.

"And whither would you go, Fool?" his mother asked him. "Why, the wolves would devour you!"

But the Fool was always singing the same refrain: "I will go, I will go!"

His mother saw that she could do nothing with him, so she gave him a piece of bread and a flask of water and quickly shoved him out of the house.

The Fool went and went, and at last he met an old one. The Old One asked the Fool, "Where are you going?"

"Look now!" said the Fool. "The Tsar has promised to give his daughter to him who shall make a flying ship!"

"And can you make such a ship?" the Old One said.

"No, I cannot, but they'll make it for me somewhere."

"Who are 'they'? And where is that somewhere?"

"God only knows."

"Well, in that case," said the Old One, "sit down here. Rest a bit. Take out what you have got in your knapsack."

"Nay, it is such stuff that I am ashamed to show it to anyone."

"Nonsense! Take it out! What God has given is quite good enough to be eaten."

The Fool undid his knapsack and could scarcely believe his eyes! There, instead of dry crusts of bread, lay white rolls and all savory meats, and he gave of it to the Old One.

So they ate together, and the Old One said to the Fool, "Go into the wood, right up to the first tree, cross yourself thrice, strike the tree with your ax, and fall on your face to the ground. When you get up, you will see before you a ship quite ready. Sit in it and fly wherever you like, but gather up everyone you meet on your way."

So our Fool blessed the Old One, took leave of him, and went into the wood. He went up to the first tree and did exactly as he had been commanded. He crossed himself three times, struck the tree with his ax, fell with his face to the ground, and went to sleep.

In a little while someone or another awoke him. The Fool rose up and saw before him a ship quite ready; and without thinking long about it, he sat in the ship and it flew up into the air.

It flew and flew, and look! There on the road below, a fellow was lying with his ear to the damp earth.

"Good day, uncle!" the Fool called down. "What are you doing?"

"I am listening to what is going on in the world."

"Then take a seat in the ship beside me."

Listening One did not refuse. He sat in the ship, and they flew on farther.

They flew and flew, and look! A fellow
was coming along hopping on one leg
with the other tied tightly to his ear.

"Good day, uncle. What are you
hopping on one leg for?"

"Why, if I were to untie the other,
I should go halfway 'round the
world at a single stride."

"Then come and sit with us," the
Fool said.

Swift-of-foot sat down, and they flew on.

They flew and flew, and look! A fellow was standing
with a gun and taking aim, but at what,
they could not see.

"Good day, uncle. At what are you
aiming? I see not even a bird."

"What? Why, this is only short
range. I could hit my mark at a dis-
tance of one hundred leagues. *That's*
what I call shooting."

"Then sit with us," the Fool said.

Marksman also sat with them,
and they flew on farther.

They flew and flew, and look! A fellow was carrying on his back a sackload of bread.

"Good day, uncle. Whither are you going?"

"I am going," he said, "to get some bread for dinner."

"But you've got a whole sackload on your back already!"

"That? Why, I should think nothing of eating all that at a single mouthful."

"Then come with us," the Fool said.

Gobbler sat in the ship, and they went flying on farther.

They flew and flew, and look! A fellow was walking around a lake.

"Good day, uncle. What are you looking for?"

"I want to drink, but I can find no water."

"But there's a whole lake before you! Why don't you drink of it?"

"That? Why, that water would not be more than a mouthful to me!"

"Then come and sit with us," the Fool said.

Thirstyman sat down and again they flew on.

They flew and flew, and look!
A fellow was walking in the
forest, and on his shoulders
was a bundle of wood.
"Good day, uncle. Why are you
dragging wood about in the forest?"

"This is not common wood."

"What sort is it then?"

"It is of such a sort that if you scatter it, a whole army
will spring up."

"Sit with us then," said the Fool.

Woodman sat down with them, and they flew on
farther.

They flew and flew, and look! A fellow was carrying
a sack of straw.

"Good day, uncle. Whither are you carrying that
straw?" asked the Fool.

"To the village."

"Is there little straw in the village then?"

"Nay, but this straw is of such a kind
that if you scatter it on the hottest
summer day, cold will immediately
set in with snow and frost."

"Won't you sit with us then?"
said the Fool.

"Thank you, I will,"
said Strawmonger.

Soon they flew into the Tsar's courtyard. The Tsar was sitting at table when he saw the flying ship. He was much surprised and sent out his servant to ask who was flying on that ship. The servant went and brought back word to the Tsar that 'twas but a peasant—a single miserable peasant—who was flying the ship.

The Tsar fell a-thinking. He did not relish the idea of giving his precious daughter to a simple peasant. And so he thought to himself, I'll give him many grievous tasks to do.

He immediately sent a servant out to the Fool with the command that he get him a cup of the living and singing water by the time the imperial meal was over.

Now at the very time when the Tsar was giving this command to his servant, the first comrade whom the Fool had met—Listening One—heard what the Tsar said, and repeated it to the Fool. "What shall I do?" said the Fool. "Why, if I search for a year, and for my whole life too, I shall never find such water."

"Don't worry," said Swift-of-foot to him. "I'll take care of it for you."

At that moment, the servant came and made known the Tsar's command.

"Say I'll fetch it," replied the Fool.

Swift-of-foot untied his leg from his ear, ran off, and in a twinkling drew from the end of the world a cup of the living and singing water.

"I must make haste and return presently," said he, but instead he sat down under the watermill and went to sleep.

The Tsar's dinner was drawing to a close, and still Swift-of-foot did not turn up though all were waiting. So Listening One bent down to the earth and listened.

"Oh ho! So you are asleep beneath the mill, are you?" he said.

Then Marksman seized his gun, took careful aim, shot into the mill, and awoke Swift-of-foot, who set off running and in a moment had brought the water.

The Tsar had not yet risen from the table; another task was to be imposed. He bade his servant say to the Fool, "Come now, show what you're made of! You and your comrades must eat at one meal twenty roasted oxen and twenty large measures of baked bread."

The first comrade heard and told this to the Fool.

"Why, I can't eat even one whole loaf at one meal!" said the Fool.

"Don't worry," said Gobbler, "that will be very little for me."

At that moment the servant came and delivered the Tsar's command.

"Good!" said the Fool. "We'll have no trouble with that."

And they brought twenty roasted oxen and twenty large measures of baked bread. Gobbler alone ate it up.

"Ugh!" he said. "That was barely enough! They might have given us a little more."

Now the Tsar bade the servant to say to the Fool that he must drink forty barrels of wine, each barrel holding forty buckets.

The first comrade heard these words and told them to the Fool.

"Why, I could not drink a single bucketful!" said the Fool.

"Don't worry," said Thirstyman, "I'll drink for all. It will be little enough for me."

The servant poured out the forty barrels of wine. Thirstyman came and drank the whole lot at one swallow and said, "Ugh! That was little enough! I should have liked as much again!"

After that the Tsar commanded the Fool to get ready for his wedding: to go to the bath and have a good wash. Now this bathroom was of cast iron, and the Tsar commanded that it should be heated hotter than hot so that the Fool might be suffocated in a single instant.

So they heated the bath red-hot! The Fool went into the bathroom and behind him came Strawmonger.

"I will straw the floor," said he.

The Tsar's servant locked them both in the bathroom. Strawmonger scattered the straw, and it became so cold that the water in the bath froze. The Fool was scarcely able to wash himself properly. He crept up on the stove and there he passed the whole night.

In the morning the servants opened the bathroom and found the Fool alive and well, lying on the stove and singing songs.

 The Tsar was sorely troubled, for he did not know how to rid himself of the Fool. He thought and thought. Finally he said to his servant, "Tell the Fool to come then, but when he comes, he must come at the head of a great army."

How will a simple peasant be able to form an army? thought he. He will certainly not be able to do that.

As soon as the Fool heard the Tsar's command, he was much alarmed.

"Now I am quite lost," said he. "You have helped me more than once, my friends, but it is plain that nothing can be done now."

"You're a pretty fellow," said Woodman. "Why, you've forgotten me, haven't you?"

When the servant came and told the Fool the Tsar's command, the Fool said, "Agreed. But if the Tsar, even after this, should refuse me his daughter, I will conquer his whole tsardom."

At night Woodman went out into the fields, took his bundle of wood, and began scattering the sticks far and wide. Immediately, countless soldiers appeared.

In the morning, the Tsar saw the army, and was terrified. In all haste he sent precious ornaments and rich robes to the Fool, and then he sent his servant to lead him into the court to marry the Tsarevna.

The costly ornaments and rich robes made the Fool more handsome than words can tell. He wedded the Tsarevna, and received a large wedding gift.

In time, all of the court agreed he was clever and witty. The Tsar and the Tsarista grew very fond of him, and the Tsarevna lived with him all her life and loved him as the apple of her eye.

A Note About the Story

The Fool of the World and the Flying Ship is a tale that has come to us from a rich tradition of storytelling. There exist countless written variations, each version as unique as the people who recorded it. With the help of Patricia Gauch, editorial director of Philomel Books, I chose a version of this tale from the *Skazki of Polevoi*. The *skazki,* or stories, were selected from a collection of tales by Aleksandr Afanasev and crafted by Petr Nikolaevich Polevoi (1839-1902), a well-known historian, archaeologist, and Shakespearean scholar. The resulting collection of fairy tales was published at St. Petersburg in 1874 under the title *Narodnuiya Russkiya Skazki* (Popular Russian Folktales).

I have taken some liberties in my interpretation of the characters, but the editing of the story was minimal as we tried to preserve the true flavor of the original text. I hope you enjoy this very old and wonderful tale.

—*Christopher Denise*